Outside the Box

Like a Family

Karin Anderson

Publishing Credits

Rachelle Cracchiolo, M.S.Ed., *Publisher*
Conni Medina, M.A.Ed., *Managing Editor*
Nika Fabienke, Ed.D., *Series Developer*
June Kikuchi, *Content Director*
John Leach, *Assistant Editor*
Kevin Pham, *Graphic Designer*

Image Credits: p.11: Joseph Sohm/Shutterstock; all other images from iStock and/or Shutterstock.

Library of Congress Cataloging-in-Publication Data

Names: Anderson, Karin, author.
Title: Outside the box : like a family / Karin Anderson.
Description: Huntington Beach, CA : Teacher Created Materials, [2018] | Audience: K to Grade 3.
Identifiers: LCCN 2017026887 (print) | LCCN 2017053699 (ebook) | ISBN 9781425853273 (eBook) | ISBN 9781425849535 (pbk.)
Subjects: LCSH: Families--Juvenile literature. | Interpersonal relations--Juvenile literature.
Classification: LCC HQ744 (ebook) | LCC HQ744 .A823 2018 (print) | DDC 306.85--dc23
LC record available at https://lccn.loc.gov/2017026887

Teacher Created Materials
5301 Oceanus Drive
Huntington Beach, CA 92649-1030
http://www.tcmpub.com

ISBN 978-1-4258-4953-5

Printed in China 51497

family

This is a family.
This is a big family.

This is a family.
This is a small family.

This is a family.
I see a boy.
I see his stepmom.

This is a family.
I see a grandpa.
I see a grandma.

Friends can be like a family.
This is a class.

A class is like a school family.

A team can be like a family.
This is a team.

A team is like a sports family.

A community can be like a family. This is a group of friends.

A community is like a neighborhood family.

There are many kinds of families.

Who is like a family to you?

Glossary

class

community

family

team